AMERICAN LEGENDS™

Paul Bunyan

Marianne Johnston

The Rosen Publishing Group's
PowerKids Press™
New York

Published in 2001 by The Rosen Publishing Group, Inc.
29 East 21st Street, New York, NY 10010

First Edition

Book Design: Michael de Guzman

Photo Credits: p. 4 © N. Carter/North Wind Picture Archives; pp. 8, 11, 12, 20 © North Wind Picture Archives; p. 7 © Jim Cummins/FPG International; pp. 15, 16 by Tim Hall; p. 19 © Phil Schermeister/CORBIS.

Johnston, Marianne.
    Paul Bunyan / Marianne Johnston.
      p. cm.— (American legends)
    Includes index.
    Summary: This book relates stories of the legendary Paul Bunyan, the created hero of the loggers who made life in the logging camps less boring.
    ISBN 0-8239-5580-X
    1.Bunyan, Paul, (Legendary character)—Juvenile literature. 2. Loggers—United States—Juvenile literature. 3. Folklore—United States. [1. Bunyan, Paul, (Legendary character). 2. Loggers. 3. Folklore—United States.] I. Title. II. Series.
2000
398.2'0973—dc21

Manufactured in the United States of America

Contents

This huge statue of Paul Bunyan faces the Penobscot River in Bangor, Maine. Stories about Paul say that he made many lakes and mountains, including the Great Lakes, Puget Sound, and the Black Hills.

Paul Bunyan Carves the Land

Have you ever wondered how the Grand Canyon was made? Some people say it was created by a giant man named Paul Bunyan. The story says that he once walked across Arizona carrying a huge ax. The ax became so heavy that he let it drag along the ground. The ax carved out the Grand Canyon!

Some people even say that Paul Bunyan built Niagara Falls. It is also said that Paul and some friends made the Rocky Mountains! Stories like these have made the **legend** of Paul Bunyan known all across North America.

What Is a Legend?

A legend is a story that has been handed down through the years. Sometimes legends are based on real people. Sometimes they are made up. Paul Bunyan is an example of one that was probably made up. It is likely that he never really existed.

In the 1800s, many people in the American Midwest and Canada worked as **loggers**. Loggers are people whose work is cutting down trees. The **legendary** Paul Bunyan is said to be the loggers' hero. According to legend, he was the strongest logger there ever was. The stories the loggers told about Paul grew more unreal with each telling. The loggers were excited by the idea of Paul Bunyan. They wanted to be strong like this legendary logger.

Most people enjoy reading and hearing about legends because they are fun and interesting. Legends can be based on real people or events. They can also be entirely made up. The legend of Paul Bunyan was probably made up.

Many loggers, like these in Minnesota, worked long, hard days chopping down trees. Most likely the legend of the strong and sturdy Paul Bunyan helped loggers deal with their difficult lives in the logging camps.

Life of a Logger

Loggers led hard lives. They worked long days deep in lonely forests. They lived in small log cabins called **shanties**. They had beds made of boards and straw. The loggers did not have machines to cut the trees back then. They used handheld axes and saws. Some of the trees they had to cut down were taller than a 10-story building!

Loggers usually cut trees down in the winter. They cut them into pieces, or logs. Loggers used **oxen**, mules, or horses to drag the logs to a frozen river. In the springtime, when the snow and ice melted, they floated the logs down the river to the **sawmill**. At the sawmill, big saws cut the logs into **lumber**, or boards. The boards could be used to build things.

Was There a Real Paul Bunyan?

No one knows if there ever was a real Paul Bunyan. Some say the legend started in Wisconsin in the 1850s. Others say the legend of Paul Bunyan is based on a real man. This man was a boss in the logging camps of Michigan around the year 1900.

Paul's birthplace is also unclear. People in Maine, Michigan, Wisconsin, and Minnesota all claim that Paul Bunyan was born in their state. Some stories say he was not from the United States at all, but from Canada!

Loggers in Minnesota in the 1890s are pictured here stacking a load of logs. Many people believe that Paul Bunyan was born in Minnesota.

Loggers in the 1800s started to tell stories about Paul Bunyan to make their lives in the logging camps more exciting. In the early 1900s, many of these stories began to be printed in newspapers, magazines, and books.

The Legend Grows

At first Paul Bunyan stories were just passed around by word of mouth in the logging camps during the 1800s. The loggers told stories to make life in the logging camps less boring. After they finished a logging job, loggers took the Bunyan stories they had heard back to their home states.

Paul's fame grew in 1910. The *Detroit News-Tribune*, a Michigan newspaper, was the first to print a Paul Bunyan story. In 1914, The Red River Lumber Company of Minnesota made Paul even more famous. They printed many stories about him in booklets to help sell their lumber. Then stories about Paul started to show up in magazines, poems, and books all across North America.

Paul Bunyan As a Baby

Legend says that when Paul was a baby, he was too big to sleep in his parents' farmhouse. His cradle was so big that his parents were not strong enough to rock it. Paul's father had an idea. He found a ship to lower Paul's giant cradle into the Atlantic Ocean. This way the waves could rock the huge baby to sleep! The end of the story says that Paul's huge cradle rocked so hard that it made a **tidal wave** that swept away some villages along the coast of Maine.

Legend says that his father put Paul's giant cradle into the ocean so it would rock baby Paul to sleep. One story says that his cradle rocked so hard it made a tidal wave and destroyed some villages in Maine.

Another legend about Paul says he saved a woman who had fallen into a river and was headed toward a waterfall. He threw some trees and hills into the river to block it up and stop its flow.

Paul Grows Into a Giant

The stories say that Paul grew to be a big, tall giant. One story says that he grew so tall that he had to use a pine tree to comb his beard. Another legend tells about a woman, Hattie, who fell into a river. She was floating toward a dangerous waterfall. Paul threw mountains and trees into the river to block it up. This stopped the river water from running. Hattie was saved. She was a giant like Paul. The story says that Paul and Hattie ended up getting married one week later.

Babe, the Blue Ox

Loggers used strong oxen, mules, or horses to haul heavy logs through the forest. The loggers who told Paul Bunyan stories created an imaginary ox, named Babe, to be Paul's pet. Loggers told stories of how Paul dug giant holes and filled them with water so Babe could drink from them. Some people say that this is how the Great Lakes were made. It is said that some of the lakes in Wisconsin and Minnesota were made by Babe's giant hoofprints.

Babe was supposed to be so big that the space between his eyes was as wide as 42 ax handles laid end to end. Loggers said that one winter, blue snow fell from the sky. Babe took a nap in the blue snow. When he woke up, his white coat had turned blue!

This statue of Babe is located in Bemidji, Minnesota. Legend says that Babe made some of the lakes in Minnesota and Wisconsin with his hoofprints.

In 1800, loggers try to clear up a log jam on a river. At that time, many people thought the supply of trees in North America was endless. Today we know we have to replace the trees we cut down by planting new ones.

Logging Then and Now

In the 1850s, large areas of the west were just being settled by **pioneers**. These pioneers used the wood from the forests to build new towns. Many people thought there would always be plenty of trees. They thought they could keep cutting down trees and not worry about planting new ones.

Today, we have fewer forests than we did in the 1800s. We know now that logging can harm wildlife and nature. In Paul's day, many people wanted to **conquer** nature. Now most people want to **preserve**, or save, our forests.

21

Paul Bunyan Today

Even today, stories of Paul Bunyan are still told around campfires. Books about his many legends continue to be printed. Restaurants, motels, and stores all across North America are named after Paul. Many of these businesses display giant statues of him. Some Midwestern towns **commemorate** the logging period with festivals called Paul Bunyan Days.

In Klamath, California, huge statues of Paul Bunyan and Babe, the Blue Ox stand in a part of the Redwood National Park. The statue of Paul is almost 50 feet (15.2 m) tall. In 1996, the United States Postal Service even made a stamp to honor Paul Bunyan. One thing that is true is that the legend of Paul Bunyan lives on today.

Glossary

commemorate (kuh-MEH-muh-rayt) To remember something or someone with an event or celebration.

conquer (KON-ker) To overcome or get the better of something.

legend (LEH-jend) A story passed down through the years that many people believe.

legendary (LEH-jen-der-ee) To be famous and important.

loggers (LAH-gerz) People who cut down trees as a job.

lumber (LUM-ber) Wood from a tree that is used for building.

oxen (AHK-sen) Full-grown male cattle that are used to pull loads.

pioneers (py-uh-NEERS) The first people to settle in a new area.

preserve (pruh-ZURV) To keep something safe from abuse and harmful weather.

sawmill (SAW-mil) A building where trees are sawed into boards.

shanties (SHAN-teez) Roughly built huts or shacks.

tidal wave (TY-dul WAYV) An unusually high wave.

Index

A
ax, 5, 9, 18

B
Babe, the Blue Ox,
    18, 22

D
Detroit News-Tribune,
    13

F
festivals, 22
forests, 9, 18, 21

H
Hattie, 17
hero, 6

L
legend, 5, 6, 10, 14,
    17, 22
loggers, 6, 9, 13, 18
logging camps, 10,
    13
lumber, 9, 13

P
pioneers, 21

R
Red River Lumber
    Company, 13

S
sawmill, 9
shanties, 9

T
tidal wave, 14

Web Sites

To learn more about Paul Bunyan, check out these Web sites:
http://www.roadsideamerica.com/set/bunylist.html
http://www.usps.gov/kids/stompfeature21.html